378

D1594876

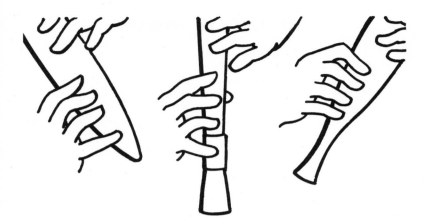

Playing & Composing on the RECORDER

by Ruth Etkin

STERLING PUBLISHING CO., Inc.   New York

Oak Tree Press Co., Ltd   London & Sydney

OTHER BOOKS OF INTEREST

Best Singing Games for Children of All Ages
Dancing Games for Children of All Ages
Make Your Own Musical Instruments
Movement Games for Children of All Ages

For Stan, Janet, and Elaine . . .
the heart of my quartet.

Cover photographs by Stan Etkin

Third Printing, 1976

Copyright © 1975 by Sterling Publishing Co., Inc.
419 Park Avenue South, New York, N.Y. 10016
Distributed in Australia and New Zealand by Oak Tree Press Co., Ltd.,
P.O. Box J34, Brickfield Hill, Sydney 2000, N.S.W.
Distributed in the United Kingdom and elsewhere in the British Commonwealth
by Ward Lock Ltd., 116 Baker Street, London W 1
Manufactured in the United States of America

Library of Congress Catalog Card No.: 74-31711
Sterling ISBN 0–8069–4528–1 Trade   Oak Tree 7061–2080–9
4529–X Library

CONTENTS

Before You Begin

Being able to express yourself with music is one of the joys of life. You do it all the time by listening, by singing, and by dancing. But learning to play a musical instrument and writing original music for it can be the most rewarding experience of all. Becoming a player-composer requires effort and work, but the results will more than repay you. Once you learn how to play and compose you will have something that will be part of you forever and will certainly increase your appreciation and understanding of all the kinds of music around you.

Many instruments can help beginners learn about music, but the recorder leads the list. It is inexpensive and relatively easy to play. Recorders come in more than one size, but the soprano recorder is the most popular because it is the smallest and easiest to handle. It is also the easiest to play and the least expensive—only one or two dollars for those made of plastic, three or four dollars for wood. The other recorders range in size from alto to tenor to the largest, the bass recorder. These are considerably more expensive and more difficult to play, so start with the soprano recorder and you will be a musician in a very short time.

You play a recorder by blowing into a whistle-like mouthpiece while using your fingers to cover or uncover holes in the tubular body. The various fingerings lengthen and shorten the column of air in the tube, making the tones higher and lower.

Unlike more complex instruments, such as the piano, the recorder can play only one note at a time. This makes it an ideal instrument for starting to compose music. Creating a simple melody line is all you need to do to be a recorder player-composer. You don't have to worry about an accompaniment or anything else, as you do when you write music for most other instruments.

The songflute is an imitation of the recorder and you play it in much the same way. It is made of plastic and does not have a removable mouthpiece. The songflute is even less expensive than the recorder. Because of its lower cost and greater durability, and because its smaller size fits small hands easily and comfortably, the songflute is popular as a beginning instrument for children in the primary grades in school. Both instruments have the attraction of being light and small enough to be taken outdoors easily or away on vacation or on visits to family and friends. That adds to the fun you can have once you get started playing and composing.

Throughout this book, the instructions and comments apply to both recorders and songflutes, unless otherwise indicated.

If you follow the directions carefully and practice the tunes that accompany each new note, they will help you to become a very good recorder player. If you compose your own tunes as you learn the new notes, you will become a better musician and have more fun doing it. By composing you learn more about music itself. You learn to appreciate the amount of work that goes into composing and recognize that effort when you hear music written by others. You learn a great deal about reading other composers' music when you write your own. Most of all, you add to your practicing enjoyment by playing your own music and learning new notes that way.

When you select the recorder as the instrument you want to play and for which you want to compose, you are choosing an instrument with a long and respected history, one that will give you many hours of pure pleasure. Enjoy every minute of it!

1. Experimenting with the Recorder

Pick up the recorder and see what kinds of sounds it makes. Get the feel of it by blowing into the mouthpiece; at the same time, move your fingers on and off the finger holes.

First, blow as hard as you can, a few times, with all the finger holes covered; then with all the holes uncovered. Now blow into the mouthpiece as softly as you can, first with the holes covered and then with them uncovered. You are learning something very important about musical tones. Blowing very gently through the mouthpiece gives you the most pleasing kinds of sounds. When you play music that you compose or music you find in song books, you may want to keep this in mind.

Climbing Up and Down

To change the tones on your recorder, simply cover each hole, one at a time. Start at the top; cover the top hole and blow into the mouthpiece. Then, move down to the next hole, cover it and blow. Try climbing down to the bottom hole, covering only one hole at a time as you blow into the mouthpiece. Do you hear that all the sounds are almost the same? That's because, even though you are covering a different hole each time you play, you are still covering only one hole at a time.

Now try playing this way: start by covering the top hole again. Only this time, when you move down to the next hole, keep the top hole covered, too.

Cover each hole in turn and keep the holes covered with your fingers as you go. Do you hear that each time you cover another hole now you get a different sound? That's because you are not just covering one hole at a time: you are covering a combination of holes. Each combination of covered and uncovered holes produces a different sound. When you learn which holes to cover—and which to uncover—you will be able to play many notes and use them in the melodies you compose.

As you climb up and down the recorder with your fingers, do you hear the way the sounds climb up and down? Try it again and listen carefully. Listen to the way the sounds move in the same direction that your fingers move. When you uncover the holes as you move up the recorder, the sounds climb higher. When your fingers come down and cover the holes, starting at the top, the sounds plunge lower. Remember this; it will help later when you begin to learn the names and fingerings of musical notes. It will be a big help when you choose notes for the melodies you write.

Breathing and Blowing

Are you aware of the way you breathe when you play the recorder? Are you taking a new breath each time you blow into the mouthpiece? Try it: take a new breath each time you play a tone. Listen to the way it sounds. Can you get a smoother sound if you play three or four notes before you take a new breath?

8

Experiment with your breathing for a while. Can you play five or six notes before you have to take a new breath? For most of the music you play and compose, you won't have to play more than five or six notes on a breath. Just by breathing normally, you'll be able to do that easily. But sometimes you may want to hold a special note for longer than that. Just for fun, see how many tones you can play before you have to breathe again.

Composing Experiments

You already know enough about playing musical tones to start composing on your recorder. You can play melodies that imitate sounds from the world around you or from stories you have heard or read.

Use your fingering to play something that sounds like a bird chirping in a tree. You may want to use the light high tones that come from leaving most of the holes open. You can get a "tweet, tweet" sound if you blow into the recorder with all the holes open. Want to change to a "chir-up, chir-up" sound? Keep the thumb hole (on the underside) covered, and then cover and uncover only the top hole as you blow into the mouthpiece. You can get other bird sounds by changing the holes that you cover and uncover.

Write a melody that sounds like the pitter-patter of rain. For "drip-drop" sounds, cover the back thumb hole again and, starting at the top hole, cover one hole, then two, then three, and keep your fingers on the upper holes as you go. When you have covered the three

9

holes, start back up at the top one again. Your "rain drops" will fall fast or slow depending on how fast you play.

You can play a song that sounds like a train chugging along the tracks fast or slow. Start slowly, with the deep low sounds you get by covering all the holes at the same time. Keep going and move your train faster and faster. When you reach the speed you want, blow the whistle by blowing as hard as you can into the mouthpiece. You know what a loud sharp tone that will make!

To get a ghost to haunt a house—musically—let it climb the steps by covering all the holes and opening them one at a time from the bottom up—slowly—slowly—until you are ready for it to say, "Boo!" You know how to blow hard to get that screaming sound, don't you?

You can experiment again and again with the sounds of the recorder and learn many things. Composers often do that to find special sounds for their music, just as you did. Keep on experimenting as you learn more about playing the recorder, and it will get easier for you to turn sounds into music.

2. How to Play Five Songs in Five Minutes

There is a very comfortable way to hold the recorder so that each note will be easy to play. To find it, pick up the recorder and hold it so that your left hand covers the top three holes. Make sure your left thumb covers the thumb hole underneath the recorder and that your left little finger isn't covering anything.

Now with your right hand, including the little finger, cover the lower four holes. If your recorder has two small holes, side-by-side at the bottom, be sure that both are covered. When your right thumb finds a comfortable place for itself on the underside of the recorder, you are ready to play. (The songflute has a special thumb rest for your right thumb, so use it.) You will notice that each of your fingers, except for your left little finger, has a special place for itself on the recorder. Be sure that whenever you cover each hole, you use only the special finger which is assigned to it.

Blowing into the mouthpiece properly is just as easy as holding the recorder correctly. Fold your lower lip back over your teeth and rest the bottom of the mouthpiece on your lip. Your upper lip rests on the top of the mouthpiece. Make sure your lips cover the end of the recorder tightly enough so that no air escapes from the sides. But don't put the mouthpiece so far into your mouth that you are uncomfortable. Your teeth should not touch the mouthpiece. Be careful that you don't cover the little opening near the top.

As you play each note it helps to imagine that you are saying the word "too." That gets your tongue in just the right position to produce a beautiful sound. If you just breathe normally, you get a pleasant flowing sound, not the choppy breathy sound that comes when you take a new breath with each note.

As you cover the holes, cover them with the soft pads of your fingers, not with your finger-tips. This way, no air will escape from the holes and change the sound you want to play. You are doing it right when you see little round marks that the holes make on the bottoms of your fingers after you play for ten or fifteen minutes.

Finger Numbers

Look at the chart which shows the recorder openings. If you follow the finger number assigned to each hole, you can play some simple tunes right now. Remember, you need to cover all the finger holes above the one whose number you are playing. For example, if you are playing finger hole 5, you must also cover the holes

12

for thumb, 1, 2, 3, and 4 at the same time. The lines
between the numbers help you keep the rhythm of the
song. It helps, too, if you sing the words to yourself
as you play.

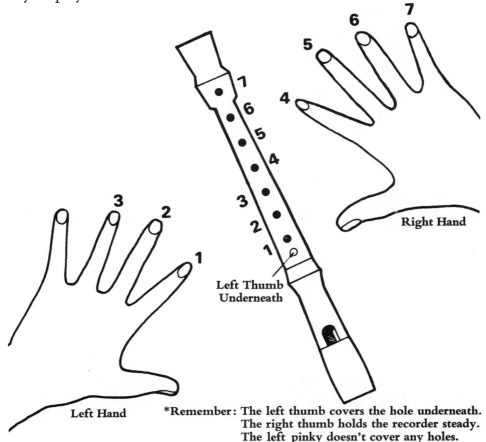

Left Thumb
Underneath

Left Hand   *Remember: The left thumb covers the hole underneath.
                   The right thumb holds the recorder steady.
                   The left pinky doesn't cover any holes.

Right Hand

HOT CROSS BUNS

| 1 | 2 | 3 | | 1 | 2 | 3 | | 3 | 3 3 | 3 | |
Hot cross buns, | hot cross buns, | one a pen- ny |

| 2 | 2 2 | 2 | | 1 | 2 | 3 | |
two a pen- ny, | Hot cross buns. |

BINGO

6 | 3   3 6   6 | 5   5 6   6 |
There | was a farm- er | had a dog and |

3   3 2   2 | 1   3 |
Bin- go was his | name, Oh |

1 1 1 1 1 | 2 2 2   2 2 |
B, I, N, G, O - | B, I, N, G, O - |

1 1 1 1 1   1 | 2   2   2   2 3   3 |
B, I, N, G, O - and | Bin- go was his name, Oh. |

LONDON BRIDGE

3   2   3   4 | 5   4   3 | 6   5   4 |
Lon- don Bridge is | fall- ing down, | fall- ing down, |

5   4   3 | 3   2   3   4 | 5   4   3 |
fall- ing down. | Lon- don Bridge is | fall- ing down. |

6   3   5   7 |
My fair la- dy. |

OLD MacDONALD

3   3   3   6 | 5   5 6 | 1 1 2 2 | 3 6 |
Old Mac- Don- ald | | had a farm. | E, I, E, I, | O. And |

3   3   3   6 | 5   5   6 | 1   1 2 2 |
on this farm he | had some chicks. | E, I, E, I, |

3 6   6 | 3   3   3   6   6 | 3   3   3 |
O. With a | chick, chick here. And a | chick, chick there. |

3   3 3 | 3   3 3 |
Here a chick, | there a chick, |

3   3 3   3 3   3 |
ev'- ry- where a chick- chick. |

3   3   3   6 | 5   5 6 | 1 1 2 2 | 3 |
Old Mac- Don- ald | had a farm. | E, I, E, I, | O. |

SHE'LL BE COMING 'ROUND THE MOUNTAIN

```
6    5  | 3    3  3      3  | 5    6  6    5  |
She'll be | com- ing 'round the | moun- tain when she |

3        |
comes.  |

3    2  | 1    1  1      1  | 1    1  2    3  |
She'll be | com- ing 'round the | moun- tain when she |

2        |
comes.  |

2    2  | 1    1  1      1  | 2    3  3    3  |
She'll be | com- ing 'round the | moun- tain, she'll be |

5    5  5      5  | 2    3      |
com- ing 'round the | moun- tain, |

5    5  | 6    6  6      3  | 1    2  3    2  |
She'll be | com- ing 'round the | moun- tain when she |

3        |
comes.  |
```

3. How to Play Notes

Playing songs by following a number chart is fun, but if you want to be a real musician and composer, you must learn to read and write music. This chapter will show you, step-by-step, each of the notes that you can play on your recorder. As you learn to read notes, you will be able to play them and use them in the music you compose.

In music, each note has a special letter name and a special place where it belongs on the music paper. You know already that when you play each note, you need to cover certain holes on the recorder. If you learn the fingering patterns for each note one at a time, you will learn them quickly and easily.

Look at the diagrams for each note. They show you which holes to cover when you want to play a particular note. When you use your left hand, remember, your left thumb covers the thumb hole on the underside of the recorder; your left little finger doesn't cover any finger holes. When you use your right hand, it's just the opposite. Your right thumb serves only to keep the recorder steady; it doesn't cover any finger hole. But your right little finger is a playing finger and it has a special finger hole to cover.

Playing "G"

To play "G," cover the top three holes with the fingers of your left hand. Make sure your left thumb is covering the thumb hole on the underside of the recorder. Hold your right hand in position at the end part of the recorder, but don't cover any of those holes. The sound "G" is represented by a note drawn on the second line of the staff.

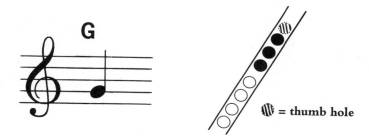

Blow softly into the mouthpiece and play "G" three or four times to hear its sound. Now you can play a "G Tune." Play only where you see ♩ ; *rest*, don't play, where you see 𝄽. The lines between the sets of notes show you where each new *measure* begins. The numbers underneath each note will help you keep a steady rhythm for each measure.

"G Tune"

17

Playing "A"

The next note up on the recorder is called "A." It is drawn on the second space of the musical staff. To play it, cover only the top two holes plus the thumb hole.

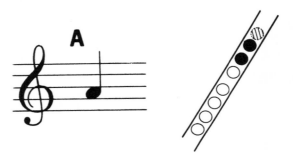

With just these two notes you can play a simple melody. Play "A Tune" first to get used to your new note and then play "The Deadly Duo." Remember, every time you play a new note, you find it in a new place in the music and you need to finger it a new way. In "A Tune" you'll find changes in the counting, too. Filled-in notes that look like this ♩ or 𝆑 get one beat (one count). But notes that look like this ♩ or 𝆑 (half-notes) get two beats each.

"A Tune"

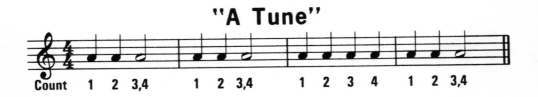

18

"The Deadly Duo"

A A G G   A A G   A A G G   A G A

Playing "B"

Climb up one more step and you find the note "B," drawn on the middle line of the staff. Play it by covering just the top hole and the thumb hole.

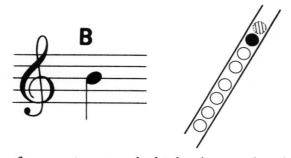

B

Stop for a minute and think about what has been happening. You have been climbing with your fingers up the recorder holes. If you listened carefully, you heard the sounds of the notes climbing up too, higher and higher, step-by-step. After you play "B Tune," notice how the notes in the next tune, the "Mystery Tune" are also moving. They climb up and climb down —sometimes they just repeat themselves. Can you tell by looking at the music for the "Mystery Tune" just where the melody will go and how you will finger it? It's a song you know very well.

"B Tune"

| Count | 1 | 2 | 3 rest | 4 | 1 | 2 | 3 | 4 rest | 1 | 2 | 3 | 4 | 1,2 | 3,4 |

"Mystery Tune"

| Count | 1 | 2 | 3 | 4 | 1 | 2 | 3,4 | 1 | 2 | 3,4 | 1 | 2 | 3,4 |

| 1 | 2 | 3 | 4 | 1 | 2 | 3 | 4 | 1 | 2 | 3 | 4 | 1,2,3,4 |

Not much of a mystery, was it? You knew it was "Mary Had a Little Lamb" even before you finished it. But would you like to turn it into a real mystery? All you need to do is compose a new ending for the song. Everyone who hears it will think you are playing "Mary Had a Little Lamb," but the new ending you compose will mystify them and make them think twice.

To do this, play the melody again until you reach the last *measure*. Then, instead of playing the note "G," play something else. You know how to play three notes: "G," "A," and "B." You can use one of them, two of them, or even three of them to give a whole new sound to the end of the song. Try it different ways and see

20

which you like best. If you mark down the names of the
notes that you finally decide on, you will have a record
of your ideas, like a true composer, and you will be
able to play the new ending any time you want, without
forgetting which notes to use.

As you learn more and more notes on the recorder,
the melodies you compose will be more interesting. Try
experimenting with new combinations as you learn the
rest of the notes. That way you will practice as you
compose and compose while you practice.

Playing "C"

Play "C," the next highest note, by using just the
second finger and the thumb hole. Do not cover the
first hole. (Songflute players, use only the thumb hole.)

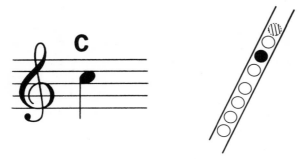

When you play "High C Tune" and "Ups and Downs,"
you will use a new counting pattern. You need to count
three beats to each measure, not four. Follow the numbers beneath each note carefully; they will help you.
A composer creates different effects by varying the length
of time a note is held as well as by moving up and down
to different notes.

"High C Tune"

Count 3

1,2   3   1,2   3   1   2   3   1,2,3

"Ups and Downs"

G A B   C B A   B A G   A
                              1,2,3

G A B   C B A   G B A   G
                              1,2,3

Playing "D"

For the next note, "D," remove your thumb from the thumb hole, keeping only your second finger on the recorder. (Songflute players, leave all the holes open for this note; "D" is the highest note the songflute can play.)

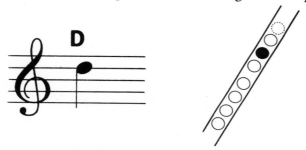

You'll find all the notes you have learned so far in the song that follows "D Tune." It is "Jingle Bells," a melody that you know, so sing along to yourself as you play. Singing helps keep the rhythm steady. Watch out for the notes that are attached to each other. They look like this ♪♩ or ♩♪ and they move very quickly.

"D Tune"

"Jingle Bells"

Jin - gle Bells,   Jin - gle Bells,   Jin - gle   all   the   way.

Count   1   2   3,4   1   2   3,4   1   2   3   4   1,2,3,4

Oh, what fun   it   is   to ride in a   one horse o - pen   sleigh.___

1   2   3   4   1   2   3   4   1   2   3   4   1,2   3,4

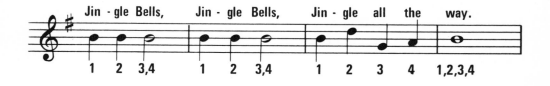

Jin - gle Bells,   Jin - gle Bells,   Jin - gle   all   the   way.

1   2   3,4   1   2   3,4   1   2   3   4   1,2,3,4

Oh, what fun   it   is   to ride in a   one horse o - pen   sleigh.

1   2   3   4   1   2   3   4   1   2   3   4   1,2,3,4

Until now, you have played all the notes with the fingers of your left hand. Now, you can use the fingers of your right hand, too.

Playing "F"

You play "F" on the recorder by fingering with all the fingers of your left hand, plus the first, third, and fourth fingers of your right hand. This is an unusual fingering, because you leave one open hole in the middle. (Songflute players: use all of the fingers of your left hand, but only the first finger of your right hand.)

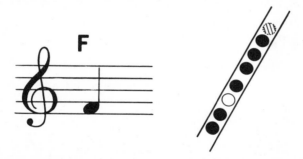

Watch the counting as you play. "F Tune" counts in threes, but "Monster Parade" counts in fours.

"F Tune"

"Monster Parade"

Count 4

1   2   3   4   1   2   3   4

1   2   3   4   1,2   3,4

Playing "E"

Move down one step and you can play "E." Use all the fingers of your left hand plus fingers 1 and 2 of your right hand.

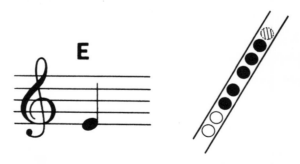

E

"E Tune"

rest   rest

"Out in Space"

E E B B G G E B D D B

E E B B G G E B A G E

Playing "Low D"

The next note down is called "D." Yes, you have
already learned "D," but this one is lower in sound and
lower in its place in the music; it is sometimes called
"Low D." To play it, just cover one more hole. Use all
the fingers of your left hand, and fingers 1, 2, and 3 of
your right hand.

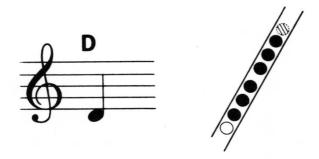

Look carefully at the music before you practice "Low D Tune." You need to count only two beats to each measure. Follow the counting numbers.

"Low D Tune"

The next tune, "Trampoline Tricks," helps you hear the difference between the high and low sound of "D." A pair of tones, like these, is called an *octave*.

"Trampoline Tricks"

Playing "Middle C"

The lowest note you can play on the recorder or the songflute is the note "C." The "C" you already learned was called "High C." Because this note is lower, it is sometimes called "Low C." Even more often musicians call it "Middle C," because it is the note found in the middle of a piano keyboard. Blow this note very softly so that it comes out clearly. To play it, just cover all holes.

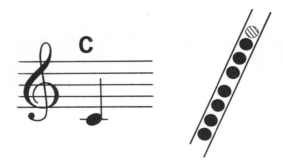

The "Middle C Tune" has only one note to remember, but in the last song, "Roller Coaster," you'll find all of the notes you have learned. Play it very slowly and try to remember each one. Let the way the notes move up and down in the music help you remember what to do with your fingers.

"Middle C Tune"

"Roller Coaster"

C D E F G G G A B C D G G

A G F E D C G A B C D C B C

30

4. How to Put Music on Paper

You can play the recorder and compose songs even though you don't know much about reading and writing music. But unless you know some of the basic rules, you won't be as good as you can be. If you learn to read music, you can play unfamiliar songs without any trouble. If you learn to write music, you will be able to set down your ideas clearly and correctly. Then you or anyone else will be able to play your compositions just as you intended them to be played.

You have learned many things about reading music already, just by playing the practice tunes for each new note. But you can learn much more about reading and writing music that will help you when you compose.

What Paper to Use

Music is a language, just as English is. But while the English language has letters, music has different symbols to learn, so that you can read it easily. With music you also have a specially lined paper to write on. This paper is called *staff paper* or *manuscript paper*, and you will use it when you write down the melodies you compose. You can buy this paper in any music store or you can make your own "staffs" by drawing sets of five lines, evenly spaced, about $\frac{1}{8}''$ (3 mm.) apart. Each staff (set of five lines) should be separated from the next set by $\frac{1}{2}''$ (12 mm.) so that each staff is easy to read.

The staff itself is really a combination of five lines and four spaces.

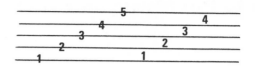

Notes and Where They Sit

Each line and space of the staff has been given a letter name from the alphabet. The letter names move, in order, from "A" to "G," and they repeat over and over. In the illustrations, you see where they fit on the staff, but they can start lower—much lower than the staff—and go much higher, too.

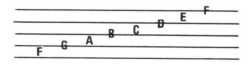

The musical tones, called "notes," are made up of many parts, all combinations of *heads*, *stems*, and *flags*. Each part of the note gives special information about it.

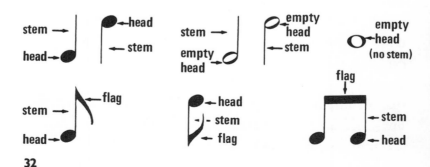

You can tell what the note is by looking at its *head*. It gets its letter name from the name of the line or space in which its *head* sits.

Sometimes the notes have *stems* attached to them. These lines go up or down depending on where the head sits in the staff.

The letter system you use for reading and writing music on the recorder is the one that uses the symbol 𝄞 called the "G Clef" at the beginning of each staff. It got its name because the place where its final curve rests (the second line) belongs to the note called "G."

Each time you write music on a staff, you start by marking it with the "G Clef," before you put down any notes. These pictures will show you, step-by-step, how to write it correctly.

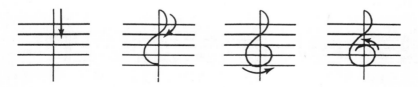

Here are the notes you will use most often when you play the recorder. See how they move in order from line to space, letter by letter.

C D E F G A B C D E F G

The form that the note takes (filled in or empty or with stems) when it is written into its place on the staff, does not change its letter name.

G G G G G G G

However, each new form of the note tells you something about how to count it as you play it.

1 2,3 4 1 2 3 4 1,2,3,4

1 2 3 1,2 3 1,2,3

Since music is a combination of both melody and rhythm, you need to think about both when you play or compose. You need to look at the way the note is written for counting as well as for fingering.

Each counted-off section of your song is called a *measure*. You can count the beats in the rhythm of your music easily if you use the *bar line* that separates each measure; a *double bar line* will show you where a song ends.

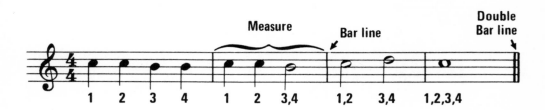

The numbers you see at the beginning of a song are its *time signature*. They tell you how to count the beats in each measure. For instance, if the numbers are 4/4, then you need to count four beats to every measure.

If the *time signature* says 3/4, then you count three beats to a measure.

1   2   3   1   2   3

Many other time signatures are used in playing and writing music. The time signature you use when you compose depends on the kinds of notes you want to play, and how many of them you want in each measure. As you will learn, each different time signature provides a different kind of rhythm for a song.

Often when you compose, you will want to use a quiet spot in a melody. In that case, instead of a note, you can write in a mark for a *rest*. These *rest marks* help keep the rhythm steady. Some are long, some short, and they each have special symbols which show how to count them.

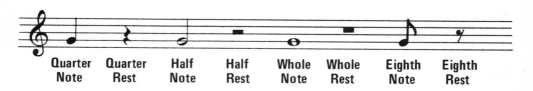

| Quarter Note | Quarter Rest | Half Note | Half Rest | Whole Note | Whole Rest | Eighth Note | Eighth Rest |

Here is a melody that combines both notes and rests. Play it once the way it is. Then rewrite it, changing the places where the rests occur. You will find that you get a completely new melody.

A composer can put together notes or rests in many ways. Be sure to check the time signature before you begin to play. Also, as a composer, you will want your time signature to be written correctly so that anyone who plays your music will know exactly how you want it played.

Sharps and Flats and Naturals

You will need one more important set of symbols when you play and write your recorder tunes. These symbols are used to change the sound of a note just a little. Sometimes you will want a note for your melody that comes just between two other notes—not quite as high as the next note up—not quite as low as the next note down. When you want to use such a note, you need to mark it in a special way.

To raise a note a half step, use the symbol ♯ in front of the note on the staff. The note is now called a *sharp*. Here is "F Sharp."

Playing "F Sharp"

Use all the fingers of your left hand, and fingers 2 and 3 of your right hand. (Songflute players: use all the fingers of your left hand, and finger 2 of your right hand.)

37

F Sharp

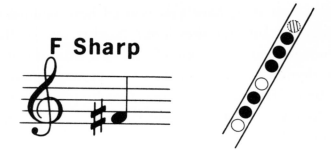

If you want to change the "F" note to "F Sharp" only once or twice in a song, then just write the *sharp* symbol next to those special notes. (These markings are called *accidentals*.)

However, when you want all of the "F" notes in a song to be played as "F Sharp," you can mark this on the staff even before the song begins. That way your music will not be cluttered with sharp symbols.

Play F Sharp

No matter which "F" note you actually play as "F Sharp" (the "High F" or the "Low F"), when you mark the staff you place the sharp symbol on the fifth line ("High F"), not the first space ("Low F").

When you play "Happy Birthday" (on page 39), you will need to use an "F Sharp."

Before you start, have you noticed how unusual the first and the last measures look? Neither one of them has enough beats to count for the 3/4 time signature. In the rhythm of this song, these two measures share the three beats. The first counts one beat (two eighth notes equal to one quarter note) and the last measure counts the other two beats (one half note equals two quarter notes). So it comes out even after all!

This sharing of measures' beats happens often in music. It makes for some interesting rhythms and melodies. The beginning measure is called the *pick-up*. Try one in your next composition. Just make sure that your first and last measures add up to the number of beats your time signature shows.

"Happy Birthday"

Playing "B Flat"

When you want to lower a note just a half step, mark it with the symbol ♭ and the note becomes a "flat." Just as with sharps, if you want to lower an occasional "B" to a "B Flat," mark it as you go along as an *accidental*.

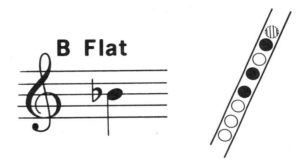

If you want all the "B" notes in the music to be changed to "B Flat" notes, then you need to mark it at the beginning of the music:

Play B Flat

When you play the song "This Old Man," you will need to use "B Flat" notes whenever you come to a "B." Use your thumb, and the first and third fingers of your left hand, plus the first finger of your right hand. (Songflute players: use the thumb and first finger of your left hand, plus the first finger of your right hand.)

"This Old Man"

*Play all "B" notes as "B flat" notes

This old man,   he played one.   He played nick-nack

on   my   drum.   Nick - nack   pad - dy   wack

Give the dog a bone. This old man came roll - ing home.

Sometimes when you mark a flat or sharp at the beginning of your music, you may decide to change back once or twice to the *natural*, unchanged note. Then you need a symbol which will cancel out the flat or sharp sound. You can see why this symbol is called a *natural*.

Natural — ♮

The next tune helps you read music with these special marks. Notice how interesting the sound is as you move from sharp, to natural, to flat, to natural. You may want to use these effects now and then in your compositions.

"Chop Suey"

F   F   F   F   F
Sharp Natural Sharp   Sharp Natural

F
Sharp

When you mark the sharps or flats at the beginning of the music, you call it the *key signature*. You write it between the G Clef and the time signature in the first measure of the music. Some songs have sharps *or* flats, but no song can have both sharps *and* flats in the same key signature. Sometimes no key signature is indicated at all. When no sharps and no flats are written in, you know that all the notes will be played in the regular way.

In a musical composition a composer shows his or her feelings. A composition is like a puzzle that fits together perfectly. Many pieces fit into this puzzle and each piece has a special mark and a special name. Don't let all the combinations of melody and rhythm discourage you. The more you play and compose music, the more you will learn from it and about it.

5. How to Compose Your Own Music

As you have been playing the recorder, you have been experimenting with composing. You changed some tunes, added new notes, and used your own ideas to give you more practice in playing. Now that you know how to play, you can start seriously composing melodies, not just for fun or as a way of helping you learn something new. You know many notes and many rhythms; all you have to do is to put them together into a song that pleases you. With what you know about writing music, you can write the tunes down correctly so that you and your friends will be able to play them whenever you want. The only supply you need, other than your recorder and your imagination, is staff paper. As you know, you can buy it in any music store or make your own.

You know there are rules that you need to follow so that your compositions will be musically correct. You know the names and staff places of the notes that the recorder can play. You know how to keep an even rhythm through each part of your melody. In the beginning, if you want to, you can mark down the finger numbers you use. Then, you can check to find the exact staff places for the notes. Soon you will know all the staff places without even stopping to think about them. Practice really does make perfect.

Although you'll want to write your music correctly, it is just as important to write music that pleases you with its melody and rhythm. For example, can you compose a pleasing last measure for this tune?

Since the time signature is 4/4, you know that the last measure, like all the others, must add up to a total of four quarter beats. First play the three measures slowly. It doesn't sound finished, does it? How would you like to finish it? Do you want the melody to climb up or climb down at the end?

Play the notes again and then sing an end to the tune. Did your voice go up or down? Did you use four notes, or three notes, or one long one? Sing your ending again, and this time try to find the notes on the recorder. When you find their places and play them, mark them down so that you don't forget them. Remember, also, to use the correct form of the notes you choose so that you will remember how many counts to hold each one.

When you compose, it will not always be easy to choose what should come next in your melodies. Sometimes more than one way "sounds good." It is up to you to choose between many good ideas. Your own "musical ear" must make the final choice of quarter notes or half notes, or whole notes and rests. You'll have to decide whether you want your song to sound happy or sad or move quickly or slowly. That is part of the fun of being a composer: you make all the decisions!

Ideas for Songs Plus!

When you write a melody that is completely your own, from start to finish, it is really an accomplishment. Sometimes you may think of a tune all at once. Then all you have to do is locate the notes on the recorder and mark them down so you can play it again whenever you want. Sometimes you will get an idea for a song if you play a combination of notes as a start: then, measure by measure, by repeating combinations of the notes you especially like, you add to it until you feel you have finished. It is easier to hear what you are composing if you play your whole melody through from the beginning each time you add a new note or a new measure.

Some composers write a song or a set of songs for special occasions. So can you. Suppose you need a march for a parade, a play or a circus. You can write one of your own easily. Music for marches is usually written with a time signature of 4/4. That makes it even simpler for you, because 4/4 rhythm is easy to keep steady. You have used it in playing many songs.

Mark your music paper with a "G Clef," add the time signature of 4/4, and you are ready to begin. As you write each measure of four counts, don't forget to write a bar line. Get the "feel" of the rhythm by counting or clapping 1, 2, 3, 4—1, 2, 3, 4. Then find a melody that "marches" to the rhythm. Use any of the methods you have used before or invent a composing system of your own. At first, try to write a march without sharps or flats. It is easier because you don't need a key signature. As you learn more about all the different keys with their sharps or flats, you will be able to write in any key you wish.

You may want to try many methods of composing before you decide on the one that you like best. You may find that you use different methods at different times; most composers work that way.

Your music can tell a story simply in its melody and rhythm, but you may want to add words as you go along. In fact, you can even start with words and write a melody to fit them. Even a nursery rhyme can help you write a tune "to order." If Jack and Jill go up a hill, your melody can climb up with them. You can choose any notes you want to continue the rhyme, and you won't have any trouble finding a way for Jill to come "tumbling after." Any poem or chant that you know, or write yourself, has a rhythm to which you can add a melody. Do it either way—invent a melody that leads to words, or find words that lead to a melody—and your collection of original compositions will grow quickly.

The more you compose, the more you will want to compose. If you are really ambitious, you can write *operettas*. Operettas are really just stories with music. Some of the words are spoken, as in any play, but some of the words are sung. Start with a story you already know. If you choose the old tale of the "Three Billy Goats Gruff," for instance, the story's characters will give you ideas for tunes. You could have a narrator who tells the story, if you wish, and then add characters who sing the parts of the Brothers.

The big brother, with the lowest voice, will need a tune written with the lowest notes; the little brother, with the highest voice, might have a tune using the highest notes; the middle brother's tune may be written with the notes in between. Think how you can invent music to match the shouting and stamping of the Troll who lives under the bridge the brothers cross. You can use all kinds of sound effects and rhythm instruments to add to the excitement of the play. You can make some of these instruments yourself (see page 53).

Writing an operetta is a wonderful project to work on with friends. You can share ideas and decide together which to use or you can divide the work. Some of you can write melodies, some the words. A few of you can play the recorder and your rhythm band instruments while others sing the songs or take speaking parts. You can even prepare some simple scenery and costumes. However you share the work, you will share the fun, too, and learn a great deal at the same time.

After your first musical play or operetta, you might start with an original story. You could write about a trip into space, or a visit to the jungle, or about your school, or anything at all. Just work slowly and carefully when you compose, so that your music is easy to read and play. Then you will be able to return to it and play it again and again without any trouble.

6. How to Have Fun with Your Friends and Play the Recorder at the Same Time

Now that you are playing the recorder and writing beautiful music, it's time to share that pleasure and join others in an *ensemble;* that simply means playing with other musicians. You can play in large or small groups; you can use the same kinds of instruments or different ones.

Get together with friends or family members who know how to play the recorder. Share the music you have composed with them and ask them to share songs that they know with you. You will both enjoy the fuller sound you get when more than one instrument plays at the same time—the kind of sound you get with a band or an orchestra.

Playing Rounds

You can play different kinds of music, too. Look for songs called *rounds.* These songs are fun to play because the first player (or group of players) starts a song and the other waits before beginning to play. At a special point in the song, the second player starts at the beginning of the song, while the first player keeps playing until the end of the song. The parts of the song echo each other. Each song has its starting point in a different place but these are usually marked clearly in the music.

48

Here are two popular rounds to help you get started in ensemble work. After you have played them three or four times and understand how they are put together, try writing a round of your own.

"Row, Row, Row Your Boat"

Player One — Begin
Player Two — Wait until Player One gets to the measure

with the star. Then you begin at the beginning.

Hold this note
for 6 beats

Hold this note
for 6 beats

"Three Blind Mice"

6 beats

measure with the star.

Count 5

Count 6

Playing Duets

You can share a song in another way. Try playing a *duet*. A *duet* is a song that has been separated into two parts, each different from the other. When both parts are played at the same time, the combination makes a beautiful piece of music. Here are two duets for you to try.

50

"Home On The Range"

An American Duet

"Clair de la Lune"

A French Duet

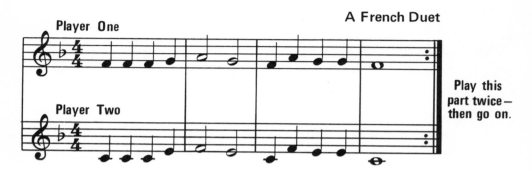

Play this
part twice—
then go on.

Accompaniment

Have you friends or relatives who can play the piano or organ? You can play the same piano or organ music together. Ask them to find some simple songs. While your friend plays the music as written, you play just the top line, the line written with the "G Clef." You will be playing the melody while your friend will be the "Accompanist" and will fill in the rest of the music. As a matter of fact, you can play with anyone who plays an instrument when their music is written with a "G Clef."

Rhythm Band Instruments

Many of your friends and relatives may not play an instrument at all. They can always join you by singing the songs you play; but there is another way they can join you, too. They can play *rhythm band* instruments, the ones that help beat out the rhythm of the music. You can buy some of these—triangles, sand blocks, drums, rhythm sticks—in a music store or even a toy store, but it's more fun to make your own.

For sand blocks, just staple or nail pieces of sandpaper around two pieces of wood. Then nail empty spools to each block for handles. Rub the sandpaper parts together and they will be as good as any you can buy.

Wood pieces   Nail sandpaper   Add handles

To imitate the sound of the triangle, hang a nail from a string. While you hold the string in one hand, strike the nail with a nail you hold in your other hand.

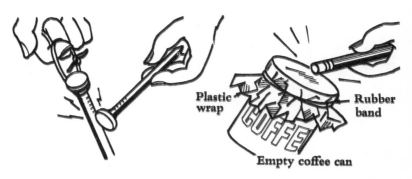

Plastic wrap

Rubber band

Empty coffee can

You can make a drum in many ways. One easy method: take an empty round coffee can or cereal box and remove the cover. Attach a piece of paper or plastic wrap or rubberized fabric over the top with a rubber band or cord. Now you can beat the "drum" with a stick or pencil.

If you have younger brothers or sisters who want to join you, they probably already know about the wonderful "rhythm instruments" right in the kitchen. They can make sounds by using two pot lids or two spoons and banging them together in rhythm while you play a song on your recorder. If you look around the house and use your imagination, you'll discover many other ways to add "instruments" to your ensemble.

If you have a tape recorder or cassette recorder, you can record musical parts that would ordinarily be played by someone else. Then, when you are alone, you can still play in an ensemble—with yourself!

7. Recorder-Craft

Recorders and songflutes need very little care. The songflute, since it is plastic, is very sturdy. So are plastic recorders. You need to be more careful, however, when you work with a wooden recorder; it can crack if you drop it. Also, saliva collects in the tube of the wooden recorder. You need to wipe it away after you play for 15 minutes or more so the wood will not warp. To do this, remove the mouthpiece, gently twisting it and the body of the recorder in opposite directions.

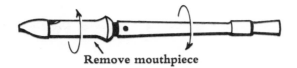

Remove mouthpiece

Once you separate the two parts, insert a "wiper" and wipe the saliva off. The wiper can be the commercial type sold in music stores, or you can make one yourself.

Twist four or five pipe cleaners together to make one long wiper. Turn up the end (about an inch or 2.5 cm. is enough), twist it into a handle and you have a useful swab.

Five pipe cleaners wrapped together

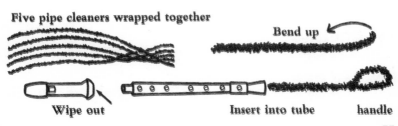

Bend up

Wipe out   Insert into tube   handle

Too much twisting of the parts on and off will loosen the string or cork that is attached to the recorder tube to keep both parts tightly together. If the string or cork is no longer in place, air will escape as you blow into the mouthpiece and the tones will not be the ones you want to play, even if you finger correctly.

If, for some reason, the string or cork is loose or lost, you can still restore the good fit. Wind as many rubber bands around the tube as you need until both parts fit together again.

Remove mouthpiece

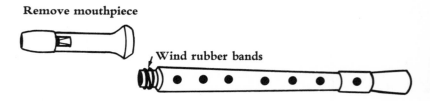

Wind rubber bands

Or fasten adhesive tape around the tube until the parts are tightly sealed.

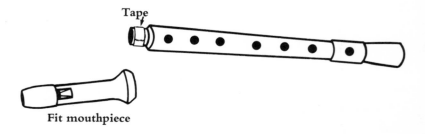

Tape

Fit mouthpiece

A Case for Your Recorder

Since the mouthpiece of your recorder goes into your mouth, it is important to keep it clean. Make sure it is covered when you aren't playing it. You can buy recorder cases in a music store, but there are many ways to make your own and the cases are fun to create.

Start with a piece of fabric 28 inches long (70 cm.) by 3 inches wide (7.5 cm.). Use a sturdy fabric like denim, duck, or terrycloth. If you want to decorate your case with an embroidered design, do it before you sew it together.

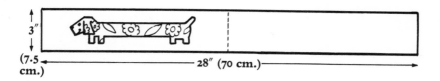

Fold down 1½ inches (4 cm.) on each end and sew each end down with a backstitch. This will be the place for your string handle later on.

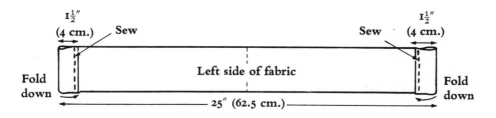

Now with right sides together, fold the fabric in half to make a long tube. Stitch the side seams until you reach the place for your handle; don't sew any further.

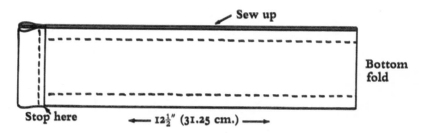

Sew up

Bottom fold

Stop here ← 12½″ (31.25 cm.) →

Take a pencil or a long, thin brush and turn the case inside out.

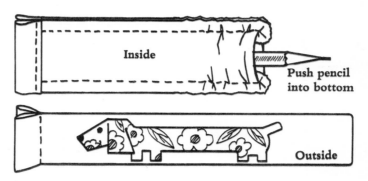

Inside

Push pencil into bottom

Outside

Cut a piece of heavy string or a shoelace and stick a large safety pin through one end of it. Use the safety pin to help you pull the string through the opening you prepared.

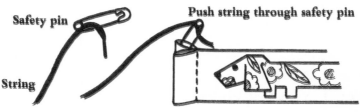

Safety pin

Push string through safety pin

String

When the two ends of the string meet, remove the safety pin. Tie or sew the two ends together, and your case is ready to use. If you keep your recorder or song-flute in this case, you can hang it in a safe place. You will not lose it and you will protect the mouthpiece.

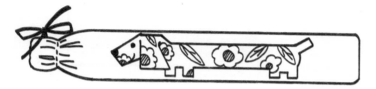

You can also make a case by using a sock whose mate is lost. Measure the sock against the instrument so you can be sure the sock is long enough. Then fold down part of the cuff and stitch around it to make a place for the handle.

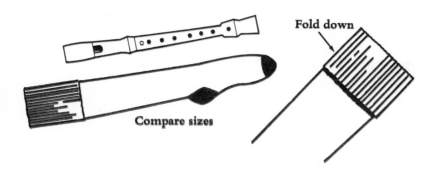

Fold down

Compare sizes

If you want, you can sew buttons and yarn onto the sock to make it look like a face or like anything else. Just be sure you don't sew the two sides of the sock together. If you keep a plastic cup or jar in the sock while you sew, you'll avoid that problem.

Put plastic cup into sock before sewing

Either one of these cases will protect your recorder and keep it clean.

A Notebook for Your Music

As you compose music, you will want to collect copies of your songs and keep them in a special notebook. You can put together a simple cover for a handmade book by using items found around the house. Certainly you can use a separate book for each operetta you write.

Use two pieces of sturdy cardboard, the kind that comes back with the laundry, or pieces you cut from the covers of gift boxes. Trim them to the size you want and decorate the outsides with pictures from magazines, newspapers, or your own drawings. The cover pictures for your operetta books might tell about the characters or scenes in the stories. You might choose pictures of some musical idea: instruments, musicians, or symbols.

Front cover

Back cover

Paste an index card or plain white paper in the middle of the front cover. On it write your name and the title of your book. Now cut plastic wrap to fit your covers and tape it in place. Put your song sheets between the covers and make sure you include extra, empty sheets for new songs you compose.

Use a hole punch or the tip of a ballpoint pen to punch two holes evenly spaced from the top and bottom of the book along the left side.

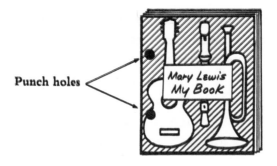

Punch holes

You can bind the book together and still be able to open it flat for easy reading by putting rings from a stationery store into the side holes. Or you can use plastic bag ties, yarn, or rubber bands looped through the holes. They will work, too.

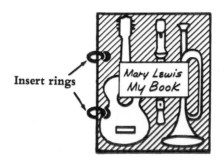

Insert rings

Music Stand

Once your book is ready, you'll want to have a music stand on which to rest it so that the notes will be easy to read as you play. You can buy a stand in any music store, or make your own from wire hangers or wire drapery hooks.

For larger books, choose a wire hanger and shape it by bending its frame into a bowl shape. Then fold the bottom part of the hanger upward to form the front support. Now bend the hooked curve of the hanger over backwards to make a sturdy back support. Test the stand to be sure your book rests firmly in the cradle formed by the bent hanger. You are now ready to use the stand. If you want to decorate it, wind ribbon or yarn around the hanger; tie the loose ends into a bow.

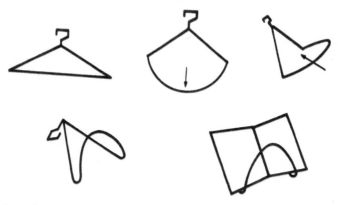

The drapery hook stand is perfect for small books or for single sheets of music. To make it, take a hook three or four inches (7 to 10 cm.) long and straighten out the part used for hanging on a curtain rod. Use this part for a back support.

Separate the prongs that slip inside the drapes. Turn up the ends of the two middle prongs and they will hold your music sheets.

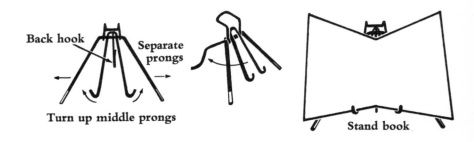

You can also form the stand by turning up the two outer prongs so they rest on the table. Bend the two middle prongs towards the back as added support.

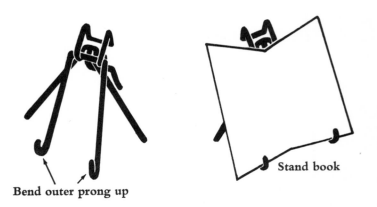

Either way, you have a sturdy, convenient music stand at very little cost and with very little work.

Glossary

accidental—a sign which changes a note just in one measure. A *sharp* ♯ will raise a note, a *flat* ♭ will lower a note, a *natural* ♮ will cancel out any signs that have already been used.

accompanist—someone who plays along with another player to fill out the music and add to the melody.

bar line—the line separating each measure of music.

beat—the pulse or rhythm of the music; the count for each measure.

composer—author of a piece of music.

composition—what a composer writes.

dotted note—a note whose count is figured by combining the value of the note plus its attached dot. The dot always gives a value half as much as the note itself. For example, ♩. is a *dotted half note*. ♩ gets a count of two, the dot adds half of that—one more count—so a dotted half note is counted as three beats. ♩.= 2 + 1 = 3.

double bar line—the two bar lines that come at the end of a piece of music to show that it is finished.

The End

duet—a piece of music written in parts for two players to play or sing together.

eighth note— ♪ or ♪ a note that is worth half the count of a quarter note. In 4/4 time, two eighth notes would get the count of one quarter note. In 6/8 time, each eighth note would get one count. Two eighth notes are attached like this: ♫

ensemble—a group which plays music together.

fingering—the use of special finger patterns to produce notes on a musical instrument. On the recorder fingering is the covering and uncovering of particular holes to produce musical tones.

flag—♪ one part of a note that shows its rhythm and how to count it. ♪ shows an eighth note, ♬ shows a sixteenth note.

flat— ♭ a note that has been lowered a half-step.

G Clef—the sign that marks the "G" note on the second line of the staff. 𝄞 This symbol is also called the *treble clef.* (See page 33.)

half-note—  is a note worth double the count of a quarter note. In 4/4 time, it is given two beats.

1,2   3,4

head— 𝅘𝅥. The round part of a *note*. The placement of the *head* on a line or in a space of the *staff* gives a *note* its letter name.

*key—*the "family name" of the group of notes that are used in a piece of music. The *key* gets its name from its most important note.

*key signature—*the sharps and flats shown at the beginning of a musical composition. The *key signature* tells the name of the *key* that the music is written in.

*measure—*section of a musical composition. *Measures* are separated by *bar lines*.

Measure

Bar line

*mouthpiece—*the part of an instrument you place on or between your lips.

natural— ♮ an unchanged note; it has neither been raised to be a sharp nor lowered to be a flat.

*note—*the symbol used in music writing to indicate a musical *tone* or sound.

The note "B"

octave—two notes with the same letter names where one of the tones is eight steps higher on the staff (and in sound) than the other. "High D" and "Low D" are an *octave* apart.

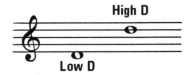

operetta—a story told with spoken words and music.

pick-up—a beginning measure that does not completely count out the time signature's beat. You add the last measure's beats to the pick-up to fulfil the requirements of the time signature.

pitch—the "high" or "low" sound of a musical *tone*.

quarter note— ♩ a note that gets one beat in 4/4 time.

recorder—a simple woodwind instrument you play by blowing into its mouthpiece while you cover finger holes on its body.

repeat sign— :‖ tells a player to repeat the music that comes before the *repeat sign*.

Repeat from the beginning

rest—a symbol in music that shows a time of no sound.

rhythm—the *beat* of the music; the way the music moves along at a steady count.

round—a melody that can be repeated endlessly. Players or singers repeat the same melody at different times, echoing the melody.

sharp—a note that has been raised a half-step.

song flute—a small plastic woodwind instrument you play in much the same manner as the *recorder.*

staff—the five lines and four spaces on which music is written.

stem—part of a note that tells about its counting value.

Stems below the third line of the staff go up; those on or above go down.

tempo—how fast or slow you count for a piece of music.

thumb hole—the hole on the underside of the *recorder* or *song flute.* When necessary, cover it with your left thumb.

tied note—a note connected to another note of the same pitch. You don't play the second note again; you just

69

hold the first note for the counts of both notes. A curved line *ties* the notes together.

Tied notes

Count   1   2   3   1,2,3   1,2,3

6 beats

time—another way to say *time signature*.

time signature—the number signs you see at the beginning of a musical composition that tell how to count the *beat*. You will always see two numbers, one above the other. The top number tells how many *beats* there will be in each *measure*. The bottom number tells what kind of *note* will be counted. In the *time signature* 4/4, the top 4 tells there are 4 *beats* in each *measure*. The bottom 4 lets you know that each *quarter note* gets one *beat*.

Count   1   2   3   4

tone—a musical sound.

treble clef—another name for the *G Clef*.

tune—a simple *melody*.

whole note— **o** a note with an unfilled *head* and no *stem*. In 4/4 *time*, the *whole note* gets all 4 *beats* of a *measure*.

1   2   3   4   1,2,3,4

Index

FINGERING CHART FOR THE RECORDER

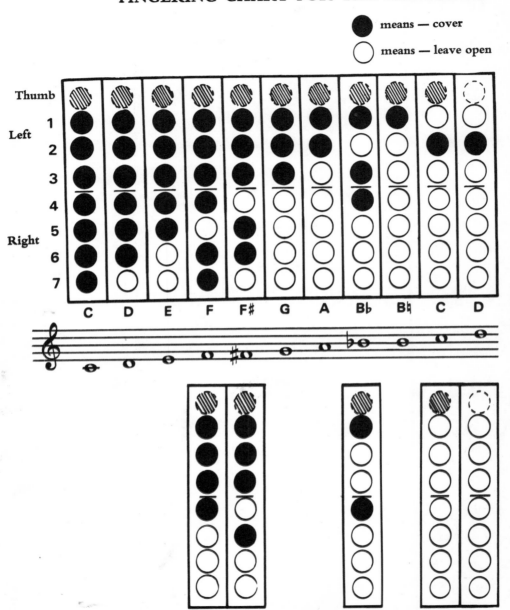

Changes for the Song Flute

72